TENNESSEE TITANS

by Tom Robinson

Printed in the United States of America,
North Mankato, Minnesota
062010
092010

 THIS BOOK CONTAINS AT LEAST 10% RECYCLED MATERIALS.

Editor: Matt Tustison
Copy Editor: Nicholas Cafarelli
Interior Design and Production: Kazuko Collins
Cover Design: Becky Daum

Photo Credits: Jim Mahoney/AP Images, cover; AP Images, title page, 14, 21, 22, 24; Wade Payne/AP Images, 4, 6, 43 (middle); Scott Audette/AP Images, 8; John Gaps III/AP Images, 11, 43 (bottom); NFL Photos/AP Images, 12, 17, 27, 28, 30, 42 (top), 42 (middle), 42 (bottom); Ed Kolenovsky/AP Images, 18; David Scarbrough/AP Images, 33; Mark Humphrey/AP Images, 34, 43 (top), 44; David Stluka/AP Images, 37; Randy Piland/AP Images, 39; Elaine Thompson/AP Images, 41, 47

Library of Congress Cataloging-in-Publication Data
Robinson, Tom, 1964-
  Tennessee Titans / Tom Robinson.
     p. cm. — (Inside the NFL)
  Includes index.
  ISBN 978-1-61714-031-0
  1. Tennessee Titans (Football team—History—Juvenile literature. I. Title.
  GV956.T45R64 2011
  796.332'640976819—dc22
                                         2010017679

TABLE OF CONTENTS

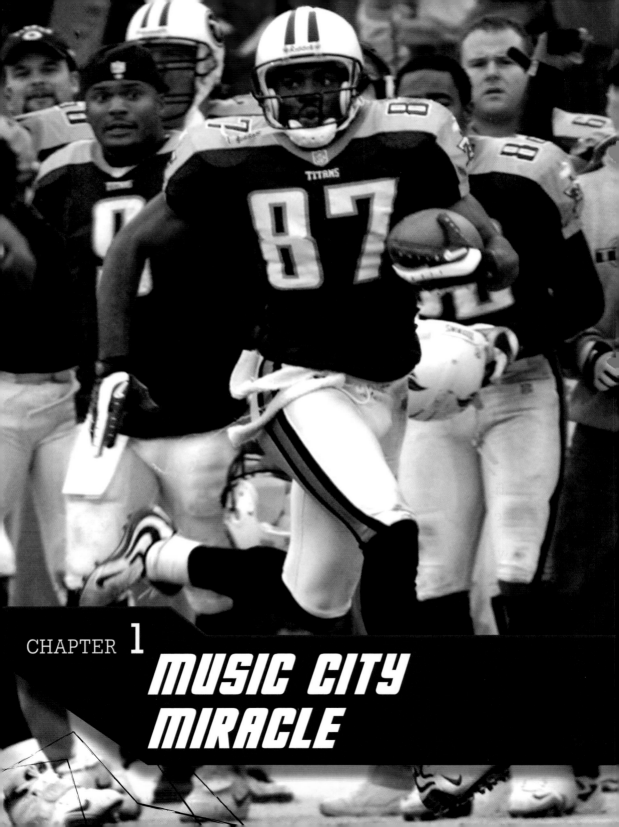

CHAPTER 1

MUSIC CITY MIRACLE

The Tennessee Titans' playoff victory over the Buffalo Bills on January 8, 2000, was one that had to be seen to be believed. To this day, it is called a "miracle."

The Titans trailed the Bills 16–15 in an American Football Conference (AFC) wild-card game. There were only 16 seconds left at Adelphia Coliseum in Nashville, Tennessee. Buffalo's Steve Christie had just kicked a 41-yard field goal. Tennessee's season seemed to be ending.

To win, the Titans would likely need a long kickoff return on the next play. They either needed to return the ball for a touchdown or take it back deep into Bills territory for a chance at a field goal. It is difficult to make those kinds of kickoff returns in the National Football League (NFL). The Titans' chances appeared slim.

However, Tennessee had been practicing a surprise play. It was the Titans' only shot at winning.

KEVIN DYSON RUNS DURING A 75-YARD KICKOFF RETURN FOR A TOUCHDOWN IN TENNESSEE'S 22–16 PLAYOFF WIN OVER BUFFALO IN JANUARY 2000.

THE TITANS' KEVIN DYSON SPRINTS TO THE END ZONE IN THE "MUSIC CITY MIRACLE" GAME. PERRY PHENIX (35) BLOCKS FOR HIM.

Amazingly, it worked.

Christie kicked off to the Titans. Lorenzo Neal fielded the ball at the 25-yard line. Neal then handed it to Frank Wycheck. The Bills' coverage team then chased Wycheck. After running to his right, Wycheck stopped and threw the ball overhand across the field to Kevin Dyson. Dyson caught the lateral, or backward pass. He then headed for the left sideline. A wall of blockers stood between him and the stunned Buffalo players. The Bills tried to recover and get back across the field. They could not get there in time.

Dyson ran down the field. He finished his 75-yard dash to the end zone with three seconds left. The touchdown needed to be reviewed on video by the officials. It was legal for Wycheck to throw the ball overhand across the field as long as the pass did not go forward. Forward passes are illegal on kickoff returns. Although the replay showed that the play was close, officials ruled it was legal. The crowd at Adelphia Coliseum went wild. The Bills could not repeat the Titans' kickoff feat on the game's last play. Tennessee won 22–16.

"We believe in miracles," Titans safety Blaine Bishop said. "This is something special. It's unbelievable."

CRASH COURSE

Tennessee had practiced "Home Run Throwback" about 60 times during the 1999 season. It was the play the team used to pull off the shocking playoff win over Buffalo. Kevin Dyson was never part of the practice. But when the Titans used the play for the only time, Dyson stepped into the starring role.

The way the play was designed, kick returner Derrick Mason was supposed to receive the lateral pass. Mason, however, was out injured with a concussion. Anthony Dorsett, who had gotten some practice as Mason's backup, had leg cramps. Coaches called for Dyson, a wide receiver, to fill in.

"As we were running on the field, they were trying to explain the gist [essence] of the play," Dyson said of his teammates.

Dyson figured it out just in time. He scored on one of the most famous plays in NFL history.

The play became known as the "Music City Miracle." The Titans' home city of Nashville is called "Music City" because it is the headquarters for the country music industry.

The 1999 season was just the Titans' second season in Nashville. The Titans originally were the Houston Oilers. The Oilers moved to Tennessee for the 1997 season. In 1999, the team changed its name from Oilers to Titans and moved into the brand-new Adelphia Coliseum.

So, when the Music City Miracle happened, the Titans fans were very excited. After all, having an NFL team was still new to Tennessee.

The good times were not about to end, either. After the Music City Miracle, the Titans won their next two playoff games, too. They beat the Indianapolis Colts and Jacksonville Jaguars on the road. The win over the Jaguars came in the AFC Championship Game. It put the Titans in the Super Bowl for the first time in the franchise's 40 seasons.

Like the Music City Miracle, Super Bowl XXXIV would also have one of the most exciting finishes in NFL history.

AFC CHAMPIONS

The Titans became the AFC champion for the first time by following up the 22–16 victory over the Bills with two more playoff wins. Tennessee topped Indianapolis 19–16 and Jacksonville 33–14. Eddie George rushed for 162 yards against the Colts. Against the Jaguars, the Titans trailed 14–10 at halftime but outscored Jacksonville 23–0 in the second half.

RUNNING BACK EDDIE GEORGE FIGHTS FOR EXTRA YARDAGE IN TENNESSEE'S 33–14 AFC TITLE-GAME WIN OVER JACKSONVILLE ON JANUARY 23, 2000.

The Titans faced the St. Louis Rams in Super Bowl XXXIV. The game was at the Georgia Dome in Atlanta. Quarterback Steve McNair and running back Eddie George led Tennessee's strong offense. But the Rams had the highest-scoring offense in the NFL. They would be tough to stop.

Indeed, St. Louis quarterback Kurt Warner played well. He threw for a Super Bowl-record 414 yards. The Rams jumped to a 16-point lead. George began chipping away at it with two rushing touchdowns. The Titans tied the score at 16 on a 43-yard field goal by Al Del Greco with 2:12 left.

But the Rams came right back. Warner's second touchdown pass came on the next play. He threw a 73-yard pass to Isaac Bruce. That put the Rams ahead 23–16 with 1:54 remaining.

Like so much of Tennessee's thrilling 1999 season, the game came down to the final seconds. In this case, it came down to the final play and the final yard.

McNair drove the Titans 78 yards down the field. The ball was at the Rams' 10-yard line with six seconds to play when McNair dropped back for one last play. McNair threw underneath coverage. He found Dyson on the move just inside the 5. Dyson headed for the end zone. Mike Jones had other ideas. The Rams' linebacker grabbed Dyson and pulled him to the ground. Dyson desperately reached the ball out. But he fell less than 1 yard short of the end zone.

The game is considered by many football experts and fans to be one of the best ever in a Super Bowl. The loss was difficult for the Titans to accept, however.

MIKE JONES STOPS KEVIN DYSON SHORT OF THE END ZONE ON THE LAST PLAY OF ST. LOUIS' 23–16 WIN IN SUPER BOWL XXXIV.

"To come this far and be a half-yard short is just a sick feeling," Dyson said. "When he got his hands on me, I thought I'd break the tackle. But he . . . made a great play."

Although the Titans fell less than a yard short, the season was the team's best in the NFL. The team began playing in 1960 as the Oilers in the American Football League (AFL). Although the team had made only one Super Bowl appearance through the 2009 season, there had been many exciting moments and players in team history.

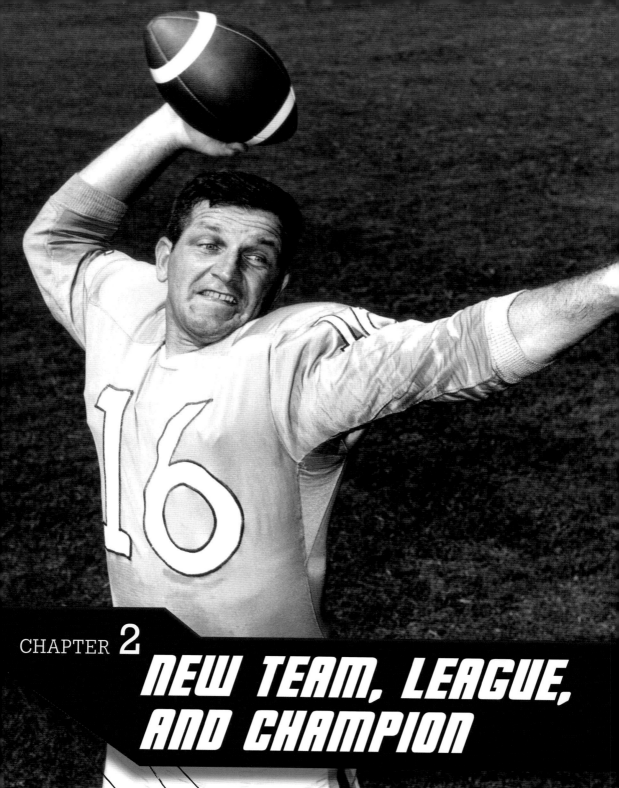

CHAPTER 2

NEW TEAM, LEAGUE, AND CHAMPION

G

eorge Blanda did not play football in 1959. At 32 years old, he had retired from the Chicago Bears of the NFL.

Blanda was settling into a new job as a sales manager for a trucking company. Meanwhile, K. S. "Bud" Adams Jr. was working to get into professional football. Adams was unable to buy his way into the NFL. So instead he became one of six team owners in the new AFL. His Houston Oilers were one of eight teams to play in 1960 as original members of the AFL.

THE AFL

The American Football League (AFL) made its debut in 1960 with the Boston Patriots, Buffalo Bills, Houston Oilers, and New York Titans in the Eastern Division. The Denver Broncos, Dallas Texans, Los Angeles Chargers, and Oakland Raiders were in the Western Division. The New York Titans changed their name to the New York Jets. The Los Angeles Chargers moved to San Diego. The Dallas Texans became the Kansas City Chiefs. And the Cincinnati Bengals and Miami Dolphins were added as expansion teams before the league merged with the NFL in 1970.

QUARTERBACK GEORGE BLANDA RETURNED TO FOOTBALL IN 1960 WITH THE HOUSTON OILERS. HE LED THEM TO THE AFL'S FIRST TWO TITLES.

OILERS OWNER BUD ADAMS, *LEFT*, TALKS WITH TITANS OWNER HARRY WISMER, *RIGHT*, AND TEXANS OWNER LAMAR HUNT IN 1960.

The Oilers and the AFL presented a new opportunity to Blanda and hundreds of other football players around the country. He returned to football with the Oilers in 1960. On New Year's Day 1961, he had a chance to lead the Oilers to victory in the first AFL Championship Game.

Houston was backed up to its 12-yard line. The Oilers were clinging to a 17–16 lead over the Los Angeles Chargers. Blanda could have played it safe. But that was not his style. And it certainly was not the style of the new league trying to make an impression on the nation's fans. Sensing a blitz, Blanda flipped a pass to running back Billy Cannon. Cannon broke a tackle. He did not stop until he completed an 88-yard touchdown. It closed the scoring in a 24–16 victory.

Cannon caught three passes for 128 yards. He also returned three kickoffs for 81 yards and rushed for 50 yards. He earned Most Valuable Player (MVP) honors for the first AFL Championship Game. Blanda passed for 301 yards and three touchdowns. As the place-kicker, he added a field goal and three extra points.

The Oilers were just getting started. After the team began the 1961 season with a 1–3–1 record, the offense started to roll. The Chargers, by then playing in San Diego, took an unbeaten record into December. However, Blanda passed for four touchdowns and kicked a league-record 55-yard field goal as the Oilers beat the Chargers 33–13. Blanda was selected as the AFL Player of the Year. The Oilers scored an average of 36.6 points per game.

On Christmas Eve of 1961, Cannon earned his second straight AFL Championship Game MVP award. He caught five passes in the game. One was

BUD ADAMS

Bud Adams Jr., the founder of the Oilers, spent his fiftieth season as owner of the Oilers/Tennessee Titans team in 2009. Adams is a native of Bartlesville, Oklahoma. He played football at the Culver Military Academy and Menlo College in California and the University of Kansas. After serving in the Navy during World War II, Adams started an oil company in Houston in 1946. He became one of the original AFL team owners in 1959. As of 2010, Adams, at age 87, remained active in the NFL. He served on several league committees.

GEORGE BLANDA

George Blanda's career lasted a pro-football-record 26 seasons. His most successful seasons as a quarterback came with the Oilers in the early days of the AFL.

Blanda was the AFL Player of the Year in 1961. That season, he led Houston to a second straight AFL championship.

Blanda might have gained his greatest fame, however, with the Oakland Raiders in 1970. That season, Blanda led the Raiders to five straight comeback wins or ties. Blanda was 43 years old at that time. In his career, Blanda scored 2,002 points and had a hand in 1,416 more by throwing 236 touchdown passes.

He played 10 seasons for the Chicago Bears, from 1949 to 1958. Blanda retired for one season. Then he came back in 1960 with Houston. He played for the Oilers for their first seven seasons. He then played nine more with the Raiders. He retired from the NFL at the age of 48.

a 35-yarder in the third quarter for a touchdown. The Oilers beat the Chargers 10–3.

Houston won its third straight AFL East Division title with an 11–3 mark in 1962. The Oilers went back to the AFL Championship Game. They rallied to erase a 17-point halftime deficit only to lose 20–17 in two overtimes to the Dallas Texans.

The team Adams created was off to an incredible start. But there would be no additional league titles to celebrate in the decades ahead. The team would get close many times, though. The team that became the Tennessee Titans still had just the two AFL championships when it celebrated its fiftieth season in 2009. It had not won a Super Bowl.

THE OILERS' BILLY CANNON RUNS AGAINST THE DALLAS TEXANS IN THE 1962 AFL CHAMPIONSHIP GAME. HOUSTON LOST 20–17 IN TWO OVERTIMES.

Houston slipped to 6–8 in 1963. The Oilers had just one more winning season in the AFL. They went 9–4–1 in 1967. A 6–6–2 record in 1969 was enough to get Houston into the playoffs as the second-place team in the Eastern Division.

The team's last game as an AFL member, however, ended in disappointment. Daryle Lamonica threw six touchdown passes to lead the Oakland Raiders to a 56–7 rout over Houston in an AFL semifinal.

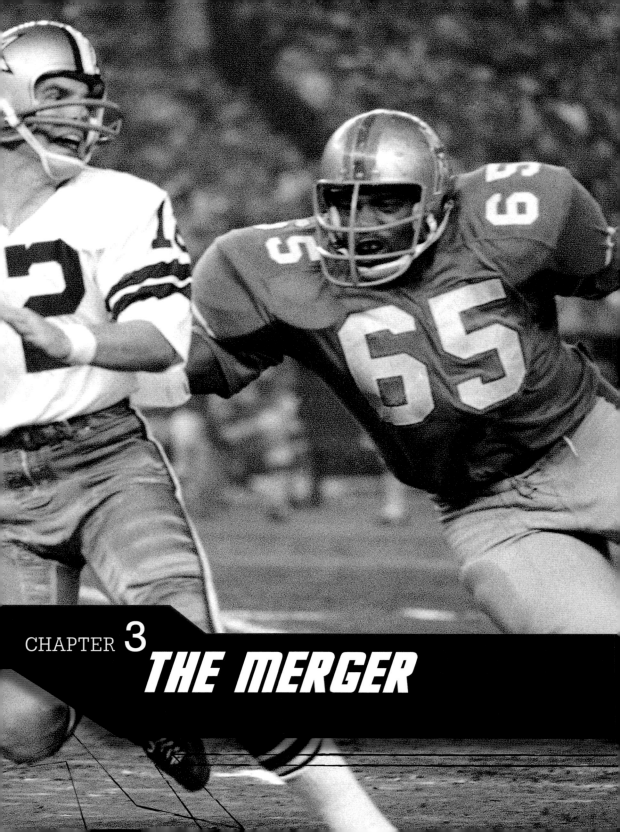

CHAPTER 3
THE MERGER

Few people saw the AFL as a threat to the NFL when it kicked off in 1960. By 1965, the NFL did. The leagues began discussing a merger in January 1965. The Oilers and the nine other AFL teams became part of the NFL through a merger in 1970.

The Oilers went through more schedule changes than any other AFL team. They had been in the AFL East with the New York Jets, Boston Patriots, Buffalo Bills, and Miami Dolphins. They were placed in the AFC Central Division when they joined the NFL. The other teams in the Central were the Cincinnati Bengals, Pittsburgh Steelers, and Cleveland Browns.

ELVIN BETHEA

Elvin Bethea provided longevity and excellence at the defensive end position for Houston. He came to the Oilers as a third-round draft pick out of North Carolina A&T in 1968. Bethea set team records for most seasons (16), consecutive games played (135), and total games played (210). He had 105 sacks when it was an unofficial statistic. That total would stand as a team record if it were recognized as official.

Cincinnati came from the AFL West. Pittsburgh and Cleveland

OILERS DEFENSIVE END ELVIN BETHEA CHASES AFTER COWBOYS QUARTERBACK ROGER STAUBACH IN AN EXHIBITION GAME ON AUGUST 31, 1970.

KEN HOUSTON

Safety Ken Houston had a record-breaking season in 1971 for the Oilers. Houston returned two interceptions for touchdowns in the season finale on December 19. In the process, he set pro football records for touchdowns on interceptions in a game, season (four), and career (nine). The Oilers selected Houston in the ninth round of the 1967 AFL/NFL Draft. He went on to play with the Washington Redskins from 1973 to 1980. He was inducted into the Pro Football Hall of Fame in 1986.

were two of the three teams that moved over from the original NFL to balance the conferences.

Before the first NFL season in 1970, the Oilers grabbed some Texas bragging rights. Jerry LeVias scored three touchdowns for the Oilers in their 37–21 exhibition game victory over the Dallas Cowboys. Houston started the regular season 2–1. But it won just one more game and finished last in the AFC Central with a 3–10–1 record.

The Oilers escaped last place for the only time in their first four NFL seasons when they won the final three games of 1971 to finish 4–9–1. Houston won just one game each of the next two seasons.

The Oilers put together their best record since 1968 when they went 7–7 in 1974. O. A. "Bum" Phillips joined the staff for that season as defensive coordinator under veteran coach Sid Gillman. Phillips took over as head coach the next season. The improvement continued. The Oilers' 10–4 record in 1975 was the team's best since 1962.

The Oilers slid back to a losing mark in 1976, at 5–9. The next season, they took over the AFC Central lead in the fourth week with a 27–10 win over Pittsburgh. But Houston played two games without starting

OILERS SAFETY KEN HOUSTON TAKES A LATERAL FROM LINEBACKER RON PRITCHARD IN 1970. STEELERS QUARTERBACK TERRY BRADSHAW TRIES TO TACKLE HOUSTON.

quarterback Dan Pastorini and five without future Hall of Fame defensive end Elvin Bethea because of injuries. The Oilers settled for an 8–6 record. But the team believed it was on the verge of becoming a playoff squad.

TOP PICK

The Oilers wanted University of Texas running back and Heisman Trophy winner Earl Campbell. They paid a price to make sure they got him. Houston traded tight end Jimmie Giles and four draft choices to the Tampa Bay Buccaneers on April 24, 1978, for the first overall pick. They then selected Campbell on May 2.

CHAPTER 4

KNOCKING AT
THE DOOR

Colorful coach O. A. "Bum" Phillips led the Oilers to their first three NFL playoff appearances. They were after the 1978, 1979, and 1980 seasons. In the process, he captured the city of Houston's imagination.

The Oilers' fans were most excited by the second of those three playoff teams. The offense was slowed by injuries. But Houston did not stop. The Oilers won two playoff games, including a 17–14 road upset of the San Diego Chargers. Houston advanced to a second straight AFC Championship Game matchup with the mighty Pittsburgh Steelers.

PLAYOFF PATH

Some special efforts were needed along the way to get the Oilers into the playoffs in 1978. Houston stopped Pittsburgh's perfect start at 7–0 by posting its first Monday Night Football *win, 24–17, on October 23. The Oilers trailed 23–0 before rallying to beat New England 26–23 on November 12. Rookie running back Earl Campbell starred in the* Monday Night Football *spotlight with three touchdowns against Pittsburgh and four more on November 20 in a 35–30 victory over the Miami Dolphins.*

EARL CAMPBELL STANDS ON THE SIDELINE DURING THE OILERS' 27–13 LOSS TO THE STEELERS IN THE AFC CHAMPIONSHIP GAME ON JANUARY 6, 1980.

THE OILERS' EARL CAMPBELL FACES THE BENGALS IN 1979. CAMPBELL RUSHED FOR 1,697 YARDS THAT SEASON AND WAS THE NFL'S MVP.

This time, on January 6, 1980, the Oilers played better. But a controversial call kept wide receiver Mike Renfro from scoring the tying touchdown late in the third quarter. The Oilers fell again to the Steelers, 27–13. Pittsburgh, led by its "Steel Curtain" defense, would win its fourth Super Bowl in six years.

Despite the second straight AFC Championship Game loss to the Steelers, the Oilers' fans were impressed. The 1980 loss was more competitive than the 34–5 defeat to Pittsburgh the previous season. When the team arrived home in Houston in the middle of the night, a crowd of approximately 70,000 was waiting at the Astrodome.

A teary-eyed Phillips addressed the crowd.

"Last year, we knocked on the door," he said. "This year, we beat on it. Next year, we're going to kick [it] in."

The plan did not work. The Oilers did go back to the playoffs. But after a 27–7 first-round loss to the Oakland Raiders on December 28, 1980, owner Bud Adams fired Phillips.

The Oilers had enjoyed their run under Phillips. "Luv Ya Blue" T-shirts were all over Houston. Phillips, the coach, was one of the stars of the show. So were quarterback Dan Pastorini, powerful running back Earl Campbell, and flashy wide receiver/kick returner Billy "White Shoes" Johnson.

The Oilers' run of three straight playoff appearances had started in 1978. The team

EARL CAMPBELL

Earl Campbell was a 5-foot-11, 232-pound wrecking ball of a running back. He had won the 1977 Heisman Trophy at the University of Texas as the best player in college football. He lived up to expectations after he was the first player taken in the 1978 NFL Draft. Campbell earned Rookie of the Year and Most Valuable Player honors in 1978 with the Oilers.

Campbell led the NFL in rushing his first three seasons and made the Pro Bowl in five of his first six. Known for pummeling defenders, Campbell also took a pounding throughout his career.

He spent his final season and a half with the New Orleans Saints. That completed a career that lasted eight years and produced 9,407 rushing yards and 74 rushing touchdowns.

Campbell was inducted into the Pro Football Hall of Fame in 1991.

finished 10–6. The Oilers earned two straight road victories in the postseason. They won 17–9 over Miami and 31–14 over New England. The win over the Dolphins was the Oilers' first in the postseason since the team won its second AFL championship in 1961. Pittsburgh, however, halted Houston's playoff run with a 34–5 rout in the AFC Championship Game.

The AFC Central Division rivalry between the Oilers and Steelers heated up. Houston clinched its return to the playoffs in 1979 with a 20–17 win over Pittsburgh. The Oilers went 11–5. Campbell was chosen as the NFL's MVP. He rushed for a league-high 1,697 yards and 19 touchdowns.

Houston beat the Denver Broncos 13–7 in the wild-card round of the playoffs. The Oilers lost Campbell, Pastorini, and top receiver Ken Burrough to injuries, though. In the week leading up to the next game against San Diego, each was listed as "questionable" to play.

None of those injured players was able to go against the Chargers. San Diego had shared the NFL's best regular-season record at 12–4. But the Oilers still managed to win, 17–14. Houston safety Vernon Perry set an NFL playoff record with four interceptions in the game.

The AFC Championship Game against Pittsburgh was a different story. Burrough remained out. But Pastorini and Campbell were back. The powerful Steelers won anyway, 27–13. The Oilers battled. But Campbell was ineffective. He rushed for just 15 yards on 17 carries.

Campbell bounced back in 1980. He finished with a

BUM PHILLIPS COACHED THE OILERS TO A 55–35 REGULAR-SEASON RECORD AND THREE PLAYOFF TRIPS. BUT HE WAS FIRED AFTER THE 1980 SEASON.

career-high 1,934 rushing yards. Houston went 11–5. The Oilers struggled in the playoffs, however. Oakland handled Houston 27–7 in the wild-card round. The Raiders went on to win the Super Bowl.

After the playoff loss to the Raiders, Adams tried a coaching change. It did not work. Houston suffered through six straight losing seasons. The Oilers fared as poorly as 1–8 in the strike-shortened 1982 season and 2–14 in 1983.

CHAPTER 5

SUSTAINED SUCCESS

T

he Oilers struggled on the field in the years after their first run of NFL playoff success. However, they began adding players who would help them play well again.

Houston drafted offensive linemen in the first round for three straight years. The Oilers added eventual Hall of Fame guards Mike Munchak from Penn State University in 1982 and Bruce Matthews from the University of Southern California in 1983. They selected Dean Steinkuhler from the University of Nebraska in 1984. They moved him from guard to tackle.

STANDING GUARD

The teamwork that is essential to strong offensive line play was easy for Mike Munchak and Bruce Matthews to produce. They were first-round draft picks who joined the Oilers a year apart in the early 1980s. They worked together on and off the field. They became business partners and best friends. Each introduced the other when he was inducted into the Pro Football Hall of Fame. Munchak played guard for most of his 12 years in Houston. Matthews lasted 19 seasons. He played guard more than half the time. Matthews set an NFL record for career games by a non-kicker with 296.

LONGTIME OILERS OFFENSIVE GUARD MIKE MUNCHAK WAS INDUCTED INTO THE PRO FOOTBALL HALL OF FAME IN 2001.

When former Canadian Football League star quarterback Warren Moon became available as a free agent, the Oilers outbid other NFL teams.

The Oilers team that took the field for the 1984 season featured Moon as its dynamic new quarterback. He played behind what was developing into a powerful offensive line. Both, however, needed time to figure out how to succeed in the NFL.

Houston added Mike Rozier in 1985 in a draft of United States Football League (USFL) players. The USFL was a league that competed with the NFL. It lasted three seasons, from 1983 to 1985. Rozier

WARREN MOON STARTED AT QUARTERBACK FOR THE OILERS FROM 1984 TO 1993. THE TEAM MADE THE PLAYOFFS THE FINAL SEVEN OF THOSE SEASONS.

WARREN MOON

Not all standout college quarterbacks are considered likely to automatically have success in the NFL. Warren Moon often threw on the run while at the University of Washington. That led to doubts about how well he would make the transition to the NFL.

Moon drew more interest from the Canadian Football League (CFL) when he was coming out of college in 1978. He went to the CFL before the NFL. In the CFL, he led the Edmonton Eskimos to a record five straight championships.

Moon made a late entry into the NFL in 1984. He still wound up retiring with the third-highest passing yardage and fourth-highest touchdown pass total in league history.

Houston made the most of Moon's combination of arm strength and mobility. He then went on to Minnesota, Seattle, and Kansas City late in his career.

had been the 1983 Heisman Trophy-winning running back at Nebraska.

Jerry Glanville had been the Oilers' defensive coordinator. He became the team's head coach for the final two games in 1985. He took over for Hugh Campbell, who was fired.

Houston won just two games in 1983 and three in 1984. The Oilers then won five games two years in a row. By the end of the 1986 season, the passing game was taking shape. Moon threw for 3,489 yards. Drew Hill and Ernest Givins both went over 1,000 receiving yards.

The Oilers were ready to challenge their rivals again in 1987. They beat the Steelers 23–3 at Three Rivers Stadium in Pittsburgh. It was Houston's first win there since 1978. The Oilers went on to start a new

playoff streak of seven straight appearances.

Moon continued to lead the way in 1991. The Oilers won their first outright AFC Central Division championship. They clinched the title with a 31–6 win over Pittsburgh. In that game, Moon became the third quarterback in NFL history to pass for 4,000 yards in consecutive seasons. He joined Miami's Dan Marino and San Diego's Dan Fouts.

In 1993, the Oilers won every game in their division and again clinched the division title with a victory over the Steelers, this time 26–17 in Pittsburgh.

The Oilers were the only NFL team to make the playoffs each year from 1987 to 1993. It was a remarkable run. But Houston did not fare particularly well once it got into the playoffs. It

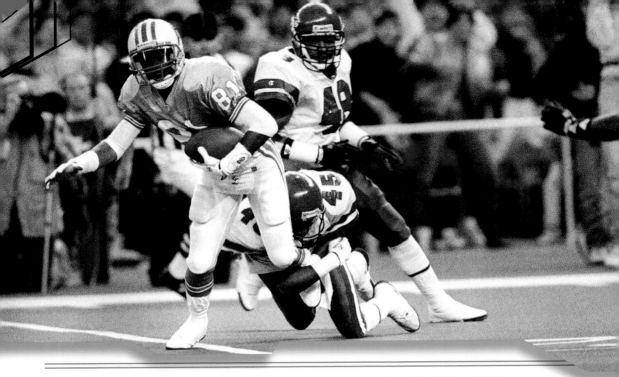

OILERS WIDE RECEIVER ERNEST GIVINS ATTEMPTS TO GET AWAY FROM
JETS DEFENDERS IN A 1991 PLAYOFF GAME. HOUSTON WON 17–10.

went 3–7 in that stretch and did not advance as far as the AFC Championship Game.

Houston suffered some heartbreaking losses during that time. One came when quarterback John Elway rallied the Denver Broncos to a last-second 26–24 victory over the visiting Oilers on January 4, 1992. The most infamous loss, though, was Houston's 41–38 defeat to the host Buffalo Bills on January 3, 1993. The Oilers fell victim to the biggest comeback in NFL playoff history. They let a 35–3 lead get away in the wild-card game. Backup quarterback Frank Reich led the way for the Bills. Moon threw for 371 yards and four touchdowns in the loss.

Many changes were ahead in 1994. It would be a difficult season for the Oilers.

CHAPTER 6
A NEW HOME

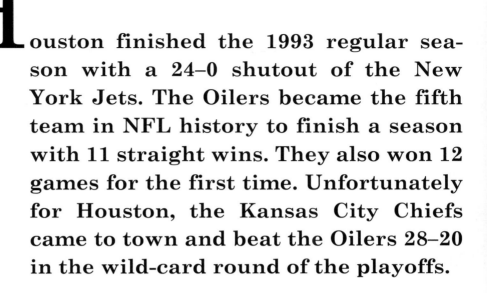

Houston finished the 1993 regular season with a 24–0 shutout of the New York Jets. The Oilers became the fifth team in NFL history to finish a season with 11 straight wins. They also won 12 games for the first time. Unfortunately for Houston, the Kansas City Chiefs came to town and beat the Oilers 28–20 in the wild-card round of the playoffs.

Quarterback Warren Moon was traded to the Minnesota Vikings in the spring. Guard Mike Munchak announced his retirement in the summer. Defensive coordinator Buddy Ryan had already left the Oilers shortly after the end of the 1993 season. He became the head coach and general manager of the Arizona Cardinals.

Those changes immediately affected the Oilers in 1994. Houston became the lowest-scoring team in the NFL. Even with a win over the Jets in the season finale, the Oilers dropped

OILERS QUARTERBACK STEVE MCNAIR RUNS ONTO THE FIELD DURING THE TEAM'S FIRST GAME IN TENNESSEE IN AUGUST 1997.

all the way to a league-worst 2–14. Houston's time among the NFL's elite was over.

Jeff Fisher took over as head coach when Jack Pardee was fired with six games left in the 1994 season. Fisher had been the defensive coordinator. He began making progress in helping the team bounce back. The Oilers went 7–9 in 1995 and 8–8 in 1996.

Before the 1995 season started, newspaper reports in Tennessee said Nashville mayor Phil Bredesen had been meeting with Oilers management. Owner Bud Adams had wanted the city of Houston to help pay for a new stadium for his team.

He believed that the Astrodome was not modern enough. It did not appear that he would get his wish in Houston. Adams began looking for a city that would build a stadium for him. Nashville was willing to do this.

Adams and Bredesen signed a contract on November 16, 1995. It said that the Oilers would move to Nashville. The NFL approved the relocation in the spring of 1996.

The Oilers played out their final season in Houston. They lost their last home game to the Cincinnati Bengals, 21–13. The Oilers went 6–2 on the road but just 2–6 at home.

It became uncertain where the Oilers would play their 1997 season. Groundbreaking ceremonies on the new stadium in Nashville did not take place until May 3, 1997. It was far too

SOUTH OF THE BORDER

The Oilers defeated the Dallas Cowboys 6–0 in an exhibition game on August 15, 1994, in front of the largest crowd in NFL history. The game drew 112,376 fans to Azteca Stadium in Mexico City, Mexico.

JEFF FISHER, SHOWN IN 1995, MADE THE MOVE WITH THE TEAM TO TENNESSEE IN 1997. THROUGH 2009, HE WAS STILL COACH.

late for the stadium to be built for that fall. In June, the team agreed to play the 1997 season at the Liberty Bowl in nearby Memphis, Tennessee.

The Oilers finished 8–8 and left Memphis after one year. But their new stadium was not ready yet. Instead, the team played the 1998 season at Vanderbilt University in Nashville.

In response to feedback from Tennessee fans, Adams also announced that he would change the team's nickname.

The team earned its first win in Nashville on October 18, 1998. It rolled over the Cincinnati Bengals 44–14. Before a third straight 8–8 season could be completed, Adams announced that the team would be changing its name to the Tennessee Titans for the 1999 season.

The Titans' new stadium, Adelphia Coliseum, was good to them in 1999. The team went 8–0 at home. The 13–3 overall record was the best in the team's history. The Titans won the "Music City Miracle" playoff game over Buffalo, then two more postseason games. Those three victories put the Titans in the Super Bowl for the first time in team history. Tennessee lost 23–16 to the St. Louis Rams in the Super Bowl.

On the final play, the Titans came up less than a yard short of possibly sending the game into overtime.

In 2000, Tennessee went 13–3 again and won the AFC Central Division title. The Titans' defense ranked first in the NFL. However, the Baltimore Ravens eliminated the host Titans 24–10 in the divisional playoff round. The Ravens went on to win the Super Bowl.

After slipping to 7–9 in 2001, the Titans bounced back. The 2002 team started 1–4 but won 10 of its final 11 to extend its season. A 34–31 overtime home win over the Pittsburgh Steelers was followed by a 41–24 loss to the host Oakland Raiders in the AFC Championship Game.

Titans quarterback Steve McNair shared the 2003 NFL MVP award with Indianapolis

FANS PACK ADELPHIA COLISEUM ON AUGUST 27, 1999, FOR ITS FIRST GAME, AN EXHIBITION BETWEEN THE TITANS AND ATLANTA FALCONS.

Colts quarterback Peyton Manning. McNair led the Titans into the playoffs by throwing 24 touchdown passes. After beating the Ravens 20–17 in Baltimore in the wild-card round, the Titans were stopped in chilly New England. Adam Vinatieri's 46-yard field goal gave the Patriots a 20–17 win over the Titans.

In 2007 and 2008, the Titans put together consecutive playoff seasons for the third time in a decade. Tennessee finished 10–6 in 2007. The team did not have enough offense, however. The San Diego Chargers eliminated the Titans 17–6 in the playoffs.

In 2008, the Titans won their first 10 games of the

MCNAIR DIES

On July 4, 2009, former Titans quarterback Steve McNair was found dead of multiple gunshot wounds in a condominium he owned in downtown Nashville.

McNair played for the Oilers/Titans from 1995 through 2005. He led the Titans to the Super Bowl against the St. Louis Rams after the 1999 season. McNair finished his career with the Baltimore Ravens in 2007. During his 11 seasons in the NFL, McNair threw for 31,304 yards and 174 touchdowns. He also rushed for 3,590 yards and 37 touchdowns.

In a statement after McNair's death, longtime Oilers/Titans owner Bud Adams said, "He was one of the finest players to play for our organization and one of the most beloved players by our fans."

The Titans held a two-day memorial at LP Field (formerly called Adelphia Coliseum) on July 8 and July 9, 2009. Fans paid their last respects to McNair.

season on the way to going 13–3. Veteran quarterback Kerry Collins had been a backup with Tennessee the previous two seasons. He became the starter in 2008, replacing third-year player Vince Young. Collins had a strong season and became a team leader. The Titans ran into a tough matchup in the playoffs, however. Tennessee and visiting Baltimore slugged it out in the divisional round. The Ravens won 13–10.

A season after they won their first 10 games, the Titans started 0–6. Tennessee recovered to reach .500 by winning eight of its final 10. Young replaced Collins at quarterback late in the season. The only losses came to division champions Indianapolis and San Diego.

The 2009 resurgence also included a dominant effort by

QUARTERBACK STEVE MCNAIR LOOKS TO PASS DURING THE 2003 AFC
CHAMPIONSHIP GAME. TENNESSEE LOST 41–24 TO THE OAKLAND RAIDERS.

running back Chris Johnson. Johnson ran for more than 100 yards in each of the final 11 games. He carried the ball 36 times for 134 yards in a season-ending 17–13 win over the Seattle Seahawks. This made Johnson the sixth player in NFL history to rush for more than 2,000 yards in a season. He finished with 2,006. Now Titans fans are hoping Johnson can run the team all the way to its first Super Bowl title.

TIMELINE

1959 — The Houston Oilers are announced as one of the original franchises in the AFL.

1960 — The AFL debuts.

1961 — The Oilers win the first two AFL Championship Games. They take the first January 1 with a 24–16 victory over the Los Angeles Chargers to capture the 1960 season title. They then beat the Chargers, now based in San Diego, 10–3 on December 24 for the 1961 season crown.

1962 — Houston misses out on a possible third straight title when it falls to the Dallas Texans 20–17 in double overtime on December 23.

1970 — The Oilers and nine other AFL franchises merge into the NFL.

1978 — The Oilers reach the playoffs for the first time as an NFL member.

1980 — A crowd of 70,000 gathers at the Astrodome early in the morning of January 7 to meet the team after the Oilers lose to the Steelers in Pittsburgh in the AFC Championship Game on January 6.

1987 — Houston lands the first of seven straight playoff berths.

1995	The Oilers reach an agreement on November 16 to move to Nashville, Tennessee.
1996	The Oilers play their last game in Houston. They lose 21–13 to the Cincinnati Bengals on December 15.
1997	The team relocates temporarily to Memphis, playing one season at the Liberty Bowl.
1998	Vanderbilt University in Nashville provides the team's temporary home stadium.
1999	After two seasons as the Tennessee Oilers, the team moves into the new Adelphia Coliseum and changes its name to the Tennessee Titans.
2000	The "Music City Miracle" extends the team's first season as the Titans when Kevin Dyson runs 75 yards for a touchdown on a kickoff return after a lateral. The play, which ends with three seconds left, gives Tennessee a 22–16 wild-card playoff win over the Buffalo Bills on January 8.
2000	The team's first season with the nickname Titans ends with a 23–16 loss to the St. Louis Rams in Super Bowl XXXIV on January 30 in Atlanta, Georgia. It is the team's first time in the Super Bowl.
2009	The Titans' Chris Johnson becomes the sixth player in NFL history to rush for 2,000 yards in a season.

FRANCHISE HISTORY

Houston Oilers (1960–96)
Tennessee Oilers (1997–98)
Tennessee Titans (1999–)

SUPER BOWLS
(wins in bold)

1999 (XXXIV)

AFL CHAMPIONSHIP GAMES
(1960–69, wins in bold)

1960, **1961**, 1962

AFC CHAMPIONSHIP GAMES
(since 1970 AFL-NFL merger)

1978, 1979, 1999, 2002

DIVISION CHAMPIONSHIPS
(since 1970 AFL-NFL merger)

1991, 1993, 2000, 2002, 2008

KEY PLAYERS
(position, seasons with team)

Elvin Bethea (DE, 1968–83)
George Blanda (QB/K, 1960–66)
Earl Campbell (RB, 1978–84)
Eddie George (RB, 1996–2003)
Ernest Givins (WR, 1986–94)
Charlie Hennigan (WR, 1960–66)
Ken Houston (S, 1967–72)
Bruce Matthews (G/C/T, 1983–2001)
Steve McNair (QB, 1995–2005)
Warren Moon (QB, 1984–93)
Mike Munchak (G, 1982–93)
Dan Pastorini (QB, 1971–79)

KEY COACHES

Jeff Fisher (1994–): 136–110,
    5–6 (playoffs)
O. A. "Bum" Phillips (1975-80):
    55–35, 4–3 (playoffs)

HOME FIELDS

LP Field (1999–)
    Also known as Adelphia Coliseum
Vanderbilt Stadium (1998)
Liberty Bowl (1997)
Houston Astrodome (1968–96)
Rice Stadium (1965–67)
Jeppesen Stadium (1960–64)

* All statistics through 2009 season

QUOTES AND ANECDOTES

Through the 2009 season, the Oilers/Titans had retired six uniform numbers: Warren Moon (1), Earl Campbell (34), Jim Norton (43), Mike Munchak (63), Elvin Bethea (65), and Bruce Matthews (74).

Mike Munchak joined the Houston Oilers as the eighth overall pick in the NFL Draft in 1982. The All-America guard from Penn State University made the Pro Bowl nine times in a Hall of Fame career that ended in 1993. Munchak then joined the coaching staff as an offensive assistant responsible for quality control. He became offensive line coach in 1997. Munchak's offensive line helped open the holes for Chris Johnson to rush for more than 2,000 yards in the 2009 season.

Jeff Fisher took over as head coach of the Houston Oilers during the 1994 season and was still in place as head coach of the Tennessee Titans after the team moved and changed names through the 2009 season. Fisher set a team record for coaching wins, pushing that total to 136 through 2009.

Through 2009, Warren Moon was the franchise leader in passing yards with 33,685. Eddie George led in rushing yards with 10,009. Ernest Givins led in receiving yards with 7,935.

Warren Moon had a chance to set an NFL record in a late-season game in 1990. But he chose not to try adding to his 527 passing yards. The Oilers had a comfortable lead in a 27–10 win over the Kansas City Chiefs. Moon's total was the second highest in NFL history behind the 554 yards Norm Van Brocklin threw for as a Los Angeles Ram in 1951 against the New York Yanks.

45

GLOSSARY

American Football League

A professional football league that operated from 1960 to 1969, when it became part of the National Football League.

contract

A binding agreement about, for example, years of commitment by a football player in exchange for a given salary.

draft

A system used by professional sports leagues to select new players in order to spread incoming talent among all teams.

expansion

In sports, to add a franchise or franchises to a league.

franchise

An entire sports organization, including the players, coaches, and staff.

Heisman Trophy

An award given to the top college football player each year.

lateral

To pass the ball sideways or backward.

merger

Combining together.

postseason

Games played in the playoffs by the top teams after the regular-season schedule has been completed.

Pro Bowl

A game after the regular season in which the top players from the AFC play against the top players from the NFC.

rival

An opponent that brings out great emotion in a team and its players.

rookie

A first-year professional athlete.

sack

Term used when a defensive player tackles the quarterback behind the line of scrimmage.

FOR MORE INFORMATION

Further Reading

Gruver, Ed. *The American Football League: A Year-by-Year History, 1960–1969.* Jefferson, NC: McFarland & Company, 1998.

Jones, Donn, Michael Mu, and Jeff Fisher. *Tennessee Titans: Season to Remember.* Nashville, TN: Sports and Entertainment Group: 2000.

The Tennessean. *Tennessee Titans: Celebrating the First Ten Years.* Chicago: Triumph, 2008.

Web Links

To learn more about the Tennessee Titans, visit ABDO Publishing Company online at **www.abdopublishing.com**. Web sites about the Titans are featured on our Book Links page. These links are routinely monitored and updated to provide the most current information available.

Places to Visit

Baptist Sports Park
460 Great Circle Road
Nashville, TN 37228
615-565-4000
http://www.titansonline.com/team/baptist-sports-park.html
The 31-acre site at the MetroCenter complex in Nashville is the team's permanent practice location. Training camp is also held here.

LP Field
One Titans Way
Nashville, TN 37213
615-565-4200
www.lpfield.com
This is where the Titans play all their home exhibition, regular-season, and playoff games.

Pro Football Hall of Fame
2121 George Halas Drive Northwest
Canton, OH 44708
330-456-8207
www.profootballhof.com
This hall of fame and museum highlights the greatest players and moments in the history of the National Football League. Eleven people affiliated with the Titans are enshrined, including Earl Campbell, Warren Moon, and Mike Munchak.

INDEX

About the Author

Tom Robinson is a sportswriter and an author and editor of educational books. The Clarks Summit, Pennsylvania, resident has covered NFL games and issues during three decades of writing about sports. He has written more than 20 books for young readers.